THE TALE OF
TOM KITTEN

❋

BY BEATRIX POTTER

F. WARNE & Cº

ONCE upon a time there were three little kittens, and their names were Mittens, Tom Kitten, and Moppet.

They had dear little fur coats of their own; and they tumbled about the doorstep and played in the dust.

DEDICATED TO ALL PICKLES,
—ESPECIALLY TO THOSE THAT GET
UPON MY GARDEN WALL

*Frederick Warne has a continuing commitment to reproduce Beatrix
Potter's exquisite watercolours to the highest possible standard. In 1993
and 1994, taking advantage of the latest advances in printing technology
and expertise, entirely new film was made from her original book
illustrations. The drawings are now reproduced with a quality and a
degree of authenticity never before attainable in print.*

FREDERICK WARNE

Published by the Penguin Group
27 Wrights Lane, London W8 5TZ, England
Penguin Books USA Inc., 375 Hudson Street, New York, N.Y. 10014, USA
Penguin Books Australia Ltd, Ringwood, Victoria, Australia
Penguin Books Canada Ltd, 10 Alcorn Avenue, Toronto, Ontario, Canada M4V 3B2
Penguin Books (N.Z.) Ltd, 182-190 Wairau Road, Auckland 10, New Zealand

Penguin Books Ltd, Registered Offices: Harmondsworth, Middlesex, England

First published 1907 by Frederick Warne
This edition with new reproductions of Beatrix Potter's book illustrations first
published 1996

This edition copyright © Frederick Warne & Co. 1996
New reproductions copyright © Frederick Warne & Co., 1995
Original copyright in text and illustrations © Frederick Warne & Co., 1907

Colour reproduction by
Saxon Photolitho Ltd, Norwich
Printed and bound in Great Britain by
William Clowes Limited, Beccles and London

BUT one day their mother—Mrs. Tabitha Twitchit—expected friends to tea; so she fetched the kittens indoors, to wash and dress them, before the fine company arrived.

FIRST she scrubbed their faces (this one is Moppet).

THEN she brushed
their fur, (this one is
Mittens).
  Then she combed
their tails and
whiskers (this is
Tom Kitten).
Tom was very
naughty, and he
scratched.

MRS. TABITHA dressed Moppet and
Mittens in clean pinafores and tuckers; and
then she took all sorts of elegant uncomfort-
able clothes out of a chest of drawers, in
order to dress up her son Thomas.

TOM KITTEN was very fat, and he had
grown; several buttons burst off. His mother
sewed them on again.

WHEN the three kittens were ready, Mrs. Tabitha unwisely turned them out into the garden, to be out of the way while she made hot buttered toast.

"Now keep your frocks clean, children! You must walk on your hind legs. Keep away from the dirty ash-pit, and from Sally Henny Penny, and from the pig-stye and the Puddle-Ducks."

Moppet and Mittens walked down the garden path unsteadily. Presently they trod upon their pinafores and fell on their noses. When they stood up there were several green smears!

"LET us climb up the rockery, and sit on the garden wall," said Moppet.

They turned their pinafores back to front, and went up with a skip and a jump; Moppet's white tucker fell down into the road.

TOM KITTEN was quite unable to jump
when walking upon his hind legs in trousers.
He came up the rockery by degrees, breaking
the ferns, and shedding buttons right and left.

He was all in pieces when he reached the top of the wall.

Moppet and Mittens tried to pull him together; his hat fell off, and the rest of his buttons burst.

WHILE they were in difficulties, there was a
pit pat paddle pat! and the three Puddle-
Ducks came along the hard high road,
marching one behind the other and doing the
goose step—pit pat paddle pat! pit pat
waddle pat!

THEY stopped and stood in a row, and stared up at the kittens. They had very small eyes and looked surprised.

THEN the two duck-birds, Rebeccah and
Jemima Puddle-Duck, picked up the hat and
tucker and put them on.

MITTENS laughed so that she fell off the wall. Moppet and Tom descended after her; the pinafores and all the rest of Tom's clothes came off on the way down.

"Come! Mr. Drake Puddle-Duck," said Moppet—"Come and help us to dress him! Come and button up Tom!"

MR. DRAKE
Puddle-Duck
advanced in a
slow sideways
manner, and
picked up the
various articles.

But he put them on
himself! They fitted
him even worse than
Tom Kitten.

"It's a very fine
morning!" said Mr.
Drake Puddle-Duck.

AND he and Jemima and Rebeccah Puddle-Duck set off up the road, keeping step—pit pat, paddle pat! pit pat, waddle pat!

THEN Tabitha Twitchit came down the garden and found her kittens on the wall with no clothes on.

SHE pulled them off the wall, smacked them, and took them back to the house.

"MY friends will arrive in a minute, and you
are not fit to be seen; I am affronted," said
Mrs. Tabitha Twitchit.

She sent them upstairs; and I am sorry to
say she told her friends that they were in bed
with the measles; which was not true.

QUITE the contrary; they were not in bed:
not in the least.

Somehow there were very extraordinary
noises over-head, which disturbed the dignity
and repose of the tea party.

AND I think that some day I shall have to make another, larger, book, to tell you more about Tom Kitten!

AS for the Puddle-Ducks—they went into a pond. The clothes all came off directly, because there were no buttons.

AND Mr. Drake Puddle-Duck, and Jemima
and Rebeccah, have been looking for them
ever since.